Little Oswald was waiting on the airport runway. He was waiting for passengers all day long. Oswald was always waiting for passengers because nobody ever wanted to fly with him since he damaged his wing.

Years ago he was hit by lightning when he was flying over the city. Oswald had to veer and swerve to avoid the tall buildings and eventually landed in a park. Everybody cheered and called him a hero at the time.

That was a long time ago. Since then everyone was scared to fly with Oswald. Even though he was very well repaired and fit to fly, nobody wanted to give him a chance. Oswald was also a bit nervous to have his first flight since the accident.

Oswald felt sad and lonely as all the other planes took off from the runway with lots of passengers.

The other planes would look at him as they passed by and tease,

"Boo hoo!

Boo hoo!

No one wants to

fly with you!".

Oswald would start to cry and think, "Please can someone give me a chance? I am a good and gentle plane and I can look after my passengers well".

One day Pilot Jack was walking past
when he spotted Oswald. He looked
up and saw his wipers swishing back
and forward. They were wiping
away wetness from the window.

"Are those tears?" he wondered.

Suddenly Pilot Jack was filled with sadness for this lonely little plane. "Oh, what a lovely plane" he thought to himself. "If I could have this gentle plane I could fly all around the world, and maybe I could help people who are afraid of flying. Oswald looks like a friendly plane and would be ideal for me."

Oswald looked at Pilot Jack and felt happy and full of hope. The mist fell off his windows and brightness shone through again.

Pilot Jack decided to buy Oswald the plane so together they could help people who were afraid of flying.

Emily was at the airport gate with her mum and dad. She looked out of the window onto the runway and spotted the lonely plane.

Emily's mum and dad had booked tickets for Emily to fly on Oswald to help her to not be scared.

Emily was scared to fly on a plane. She remembered that the last time she was on a plane she had cried and cried. That was two years ago but she still thought about it.

As Emily and her parents boarded the plane, she looked up at Oswald. He looked enormous, but he was still smaller than all the other planes. Somehow he did not look scary.

Emily looked into the cockpit window and could see her own reflection, but she could also sense a big smile in the cockpit.

It was as if the plane was smiling at her!

She imagined that she saw Oswald's wings flapping up and down, as though they were waving to her.

Oswald was feeling very excited. For the first time since the accident someone was looking at him.

"If only I could tell that little girl that I will give her a lovely flight and not to worry" he thought.

Oswald tried to give Emily a big smile. "I hope she understands my smile" thought Oswald as he waved his wipers and flapped his wings from side to side to say hello.

Emily stepped up the stairs of the plane with her mum and dad. She did not feel scared like the last time.

When she boarded the plane she could see lots of children running up and down the aisle and playing happily.

She realised that all the people there were once scared of flying too, but when they stepped onto this lovely plane called Oswald, all of their doubts disappeared.

Emily sat down in her seat and found it felt soft like candy floss. It also smelt sweet like toffee apples.

Pilot Jack welcomed everybody on board and asked them to sit down and fasten their seat belts. He told them to relax and enjoy the flight. They would be taking off in a few minutes.

Emily looked out the window and could feel the plane moving. She did not feel scared anymore and was amazed as the plane took off. She could see the buildings getting smaller and smaller.

As the plane soared up into the air Emily could see all the fluffy white clouds in the bright blue sky. She imagined herself surfing on the clouds, playing with her friends.

Oswald laughed as he swept through the clouds. He was delighted to be flying and could hear the children laughing; it made him feel overjoyed. He had not felt this happy in a long time.

He decided to give his passengers a treat and fly them higher and higher so they could enjoy all the scenery from the sky above.

Emily was fascinated as she first saw the mountains topped with snow and then she saw the clouds. Then she looked at the lakes and the valleys.

As Oswald flew over the snow covered mountains, Emily thought that they looked like lots of fluffy marshmallows and wondered if she could jump out and eat them all up.

As the plane looped in circles, it almost touched the ground. Emily could see people waving at the plane as it lifted again, a long way into the sky.

Emily imagined she was heading towards the sun.

Pilot Jack checked with Oswald if he had enough fuel to fly around the world. "Of course I have," beamed Oswald, "I am fuelled on happiness and that is all I need."

Oswald was so happy. He had waited so long to get a chance to let people know what a special plane he was. Now he had a lot of happy children on board. This was his chance to shine and to show the children all the wonderful places in the world.

Suddenly, Oswald spun around and glided over Paris. Emily could see the Eiffel Tower, all lit up.

She shouted with joy, "I always wanted to see the Eiffel Tower".

Then Oswald swerved around and hovered over the pyramids in Egypt. He showed them all over the world from the ice fields of Alaska to the sands of the Sahara Desert.

"I wish this journey would never end" cried Emily.

Pilot Jack announced that they would soon be landing and hoped that they had all had a wonderful trip. Emily and the rest of the children left the plane in such a happy mood.

Emily waved goodbye to Oswald and for a moment she felt that he winked back at her.

As she wondered whether she had imagined it, the not-so-lonely plane smiled at her and she knew that she would never feel scared of flying again.